Journey

A. R.

Copyright © 2020 A.R.

All rights reserved.
ISBN: 9798693840775

Contact: ar@journeythebook.com

Book One

To the Northern land

DEDICATION

To every seeking soul.

Contents

Chapter 1: The Seed – as it happened 7

Chapter 2: The Root – as it grew 12

Chapter 3: The Shoot – for the need of shade 16

Chapter 4: Branches – The limits are unlimited 26

Chapter 5: Green Branch – The first tribe 38

Chapter 6: Brown branch – The second tribe 45

Chapter 7: The fruit – The bait of illusion 52

Chapter 8: The soil – In the wilderness 58

Chapter 9 66

Chapter 10: The Light – The name after nameless 74

Chapter 11: The Subtle – Wisdom from within 86

Chapter 12: The companion – On how to conquer 90

Chapter 13: Slumber – When the dreams look real 96

Chapter 14: Reality – The causes of illusion 99

ACKNOWLEDGMENTS

To the wildest of my dreams, and Hazel Anna without whom this book would have been an unreadable mess of words.

Chapter 1

The Seed – as it happened

I Zmel was cast aside, being the son of a concubine. His mother was promiscuous, for the law was not in her favor. His father was pious, for the law was in his favor. Yet, Izmel was cast aside, for the burden of his childhood questioned his reasoning, his origin, and his purpose.

When Izmel was five, he met Siempre, his friend, his foe, an object that would change the course of his life for fifteen long years. It consumed his mind like a parasite, a seed that grew like a weed. For fifteen long years, Siempre slept by his side, intimate, breathing the same air, jealous, loving and kind. Izmel, in his tender age with a fertile soul and a curious mind watered the seed with love and care. The seed grew frantically, swimming in a sea of unbound thoughts, nourished by Izmel's juvenile energy. Its roots grew strong and wild, its shoots protruding in different colors - the plant was beautiful, poisonous - Izmel called it 'my Little Siempre', for his love for the plant was obsessive.

Siempre, as disgusting as it would seem had a struggling edge beneath its venomous self. A struggling soul, whose carnal desire was hidden in its pursuit of intelligence. Its intelligence reflected on earth and air – on earth, it molded iron into steel, it wired silicon into marvelous lights; on air, it sought spirits unknown, it breathed the breeze of coastal Chechua to welcome the spirits, their beliefs, colors and flameless fires. Siempre gifted Izmel with beautiful carvings of metals and philosophies blessed by its spirits. Izmel, astonished and allured, craved for Siempre, swimming high and low as the tides of the salty sea of Chechua rose and fell by the law that ruled it.

Meanwhile, Izmel sought purity, his intellect wandered to sail in the wind of truth to his essence, washing the sins that malign the toxic air fed by the greed and desires of impatient human mortals. He desired to stay away from the tree that decided the fate of his soul, his fellow souls and his non-fellow souls.

As Little Siempre grew, Izmel didn't know that it was a parasite residing in the gateway of his destiny. It sucked the blood of the child, processed it like a factory and spat out the toxic thoughts it has inherited from Siempre. The nature of ingenuity and creativity – on earth and air, passion and jealousy that defined Siempre was mirrored in the juvenile thoughts of Izmel. For Izmel, it was strange at the beginning. The staff he carried, inherited from his love towards the man who ran across the sea, was cast aside for the carnal desires he inherited from Siempre. He let it loose, stage by stage, to a point where he lost his identity inherited from his pious father and concubine mother.

Izmel felt that society was like Siempre, everyone – his concubine mother, his pious father – everyone he knew, and everyone he knew not. He was shy because of the guilt that galled his back; his feebleness bought fragility; his curiosity invited everything on his way – saying no to only one thing, idols, those freaking spirits Siempre worshipped. As dark as it sounds, Izmel was afraid of society, and he sought solace against it hiding in the blankets of that gift of immunity, the immunity that he inherited from his pious father.

Siempre not only instilled carnal realities on Izmel, it tamed him through cravings and aversions. As much earth and air Siempre would gift, Siempre would starve Izmel to crave for its comfort. In his tender age, Izmel would cry loud as much as he feared his tears would fill up the salty sea of Chechua - yearning for love, yearning for freedom, as Siempre would be lost in its worldly pleasures with his beloved little love. Siempre was sneaky, suspicious - spied everything in Izmel's household - about his promiscuous mother, his pious father, and his siblings, alive and dead. Yet, Izmel had his own secrets - many of which will be revealed, while others are meant to be Izmel's for all the pain of his life.

It was a dark age, an age that quenched the beautiful ray of hope Izmel sought with the shade of earthly desires. His ambition to turn the shaft into serpent, his ambition to witness the power of the Creator, his ambition to find the perfect love was shattered by his curiosity, his greed, and his pleasure. The forbidden tree was laid bare in the footsteps of his home. His concubine mother watched in oblivion as the roots of greed as they creeped into the house of the Pious through the soils of the land of Chechua.

Chapter 2

The Root – as it grew

The roots were two-fold, on either direction – one stretching to his groin, and the other creeping to his heart. Izmel called the lower root Ta, and the upper root Ga. Izmel had his own reasons – some reasons are known only to him, and his Creator (in fact, Ga had another name, and only Izmel knows what it is. In this book, many truths will be revealed, but not the other name of Ga) – it is fair, for what he has achieved – that some reasons are secret to Izmel.

Ta was fire, freedom and craving. Ta opened up its roots to sensuality, to immediate pleasure and freedom. Ga was flameless, pure and sublime. Ga unwrapped consciousness to a horizon – a level unseen, unheard and unfelt by humans (with some exceptions). The two roots outstretched Izmel, pulling him way apart, polarizing his mind nurtured by its impermanence, stretching his spine like the curves inside a snail's carapace curling out of shape.

As Izmel grew older, he was not dismayed by his inability to focus on Ga. He succumbed to Ta, his groins out-bursting with cravings for sensual pleasures, revealing some innermost desires to a prohibitive extent, until finally one night he saw a glimpse of Ga, which filled him with guilt that he would carry for many more years. A cat, honing its predatory skills, would play around with a little cute cockroach – watching it suffering all the way until it dies. The cat was unaware of the suffering of the cockroach, it was amused by its movement and fluttering – so was poor Izmel. Izmel was young, he was a child, and he was learning the intricacies of his sensualities while his concubine mother watched in oblivion.

The last time Siempre could breathe his intimate spirits to Izmel, Izmel smelt the putrid breath of adulthood. Siempre, feeling the heat of Izmel's adulthood got perturbed – he greatly feared the fading innocence of the child. As Izmel felt himself lost in the shades of Siempre's desires, he retreated into his maturing conscience, while Ga, holy Ga, breathed its essence on Izmel's awareness. Izmel filled with guilt and anger, casted his flaming adulthood at the seed he nurtured for years. He saw the crookedness of his dear Siempre as vivid as the eyes of the howling owls. He pushed him away with force and vengeance, yet his adolescent empathy poured through his words of consciousness, and he questioned Siempre with what seemed to be the words of maturing wisdom. When Siempre was startled at Izmel's sprouting wisdom which suggested a clear distinction between right and wrong, Izmel threw his imaginary stake, and it turned into a serpent of vengeance. The snake creeped vehemently in the house of the pious, like sperm inside a newlywed virgin, devouring every drop of nectar spilled by Siempre and every root protruding in the house of the pious. That serpent was the serpent that turned white without blemish in the darkness of the night, spilling in the guts of Siempre like the fruit of the forbidden tree.

That was the last night Siempre could approach Izmel, that was the night when Izmel saw the absolute starkness of darkness and light, of screech and silence, of debauchery and courage. When the dawn struck the windows of Izmel's adolescent eyes, a thin ray of light overshadowing the mighty darkness, Izmel saw Siempre withdrawing, crawling away from his intimate side while his concubine mother watched in oblivion. He thus saw him for one last time, Siempre, Izmel's little Siempre withdrawing like an elusive and defeated serpent, panting at its disgrace, fearful of the approaching light, a light that was too bright for Siempre, a brightness that blinded the epoch of carnal desires that withstood the time of fifteen long years on the soil of the land of Chechua.

Fifteen long years of Ta, fifteen long years of suffering seems to have ended – but the roots were so grown inside Izmel, synapsing to his nervous system bringing pain and anger, guilt and despair. Izmel's pursuit for the next ten years was to get the Ga back, and consequently the journey of his adulthood!

Chapter 3

The Shoot – for the need of shade

The end of Izmel's little Siempre was the beginning of Izmel's larger Siempre. Siempre left the seed of desire, and it grew with Ta, yet he found a void, a void that obscured his heart, a void that would haunt Izmel for the rest of his adolescence.

Pious had gifted a pair of magnets to Izmel when he turned six. Sometimes, the magnets would spread their wings away as if they hated to the moon, but no further away from the moon for the moon sticks around for its love of earth. At other times, the magnets would stick together as if they were the loves of their lives, for they can't get any closer without amputating themselves into baby magnets. Izmel spent hours, days playing with them – they were pets, living and breathing, and converging and diverging to craving and aversion. He would watch them with his large dark eyes, furrowing his thick brown eyebrows inherited from his concubine mother and think about how the world works, the nature of life, death and belonging, precipitation and evaporation – two pieces of rock that opened his eyes towards the nature of duality. His thick forehead inherited from his pious father would shrivel with waves of marvel, as if the wonderment he saw in the whispers of those tiny magnets was nothing less than the greatest discovery man has ever found. With the loss of little Siempre, with a void that grew along the distance of time, Izmel sought his pair of magnet as he wandered around the world – sex, music, dream, nature, art – a quest for the holy pair, an eternal search for his lost Siempre, a being that would fill his naked void, a search that would lead Izmel to places of interest very few humans have seen either to the south or north of the land of Chechua.

As his yearning for the pair grew, carrying the heavy burden he inherited from his childhood, Izmel couldn't resist leaving for an adventure that would decide the fate of his life as well as that of many other souls. A tiny ray of light that would reveal the essence of truth, hidden in pain and pleasure – Izmel and many others have to take these recitals with caution, as truth as sublime as it gets is hard to be felt with human consciousness.

Leaves breath the vapor of life, seeking the ray of sun, providing shade for their beloved shoots, and perishing in the feet of their beloved shoots. Izmel, carrying the strength of his adult masculinity bid farewell to his pious father and concubine mother to search for a place to the north. Like a wildebeest that needs to cross the river, regardless of the hungry crocodiles waiting for a piece of its meat, Izmel broke the walls of his household and journeyed to a world unknown, with the bright light of unseen hope shining on his tearful lashes.

As he walked through the field, with striking green pastures of the land of Chechua brushing his tender feet, he felt the chill of earth. He kneeled down to grab a piece of earth to his arm, felt its warmth, smelt its dampness and he felt the warmth of his own being from which he was created and to which he will return. The breeze of northern winds caressed his tearful lashes, the memory of his concubine mother and pious father fading in and out like twinkling stars. It was as painful as a six-week old dove leaving her mother's nest to seek the glory of life. He would look at the tree, talk to the birds, and take every care to not hurt any crawling being. He would breath the luxury of nature, so perfectly made to nourish the weakest being on the earth. He saw the sun moving in its course, the moon fading like the leaves of a palm tree, working hard to catch up with the sun, with stars twinkling in pain and hope, Izmel yearned to be a part of the law, submitting to what created him and everything else. Yet, he was far away from what Ga had to offer him.

In the land of Magua, a little north of Chechua where Izmel met Siempre, Izmel saw a smoke in the distance hovering and coating the skies with darkness. As he approached the smoke, he saw a girl, a few years younger than him who had circumambulated the sun twenty times by then, carrying the firewood to a house upon which there was smoke as grey as a cloudy dusk of winters. She was clad with the skin of a mountain goat scantily covering her bosoms for it was forbidden in the land of Magua for women to fully cover their breasts. It was the privilege for men to see them, and the privilege for women to not show them. Her hair, as dark as the widow spider comforted the skin of the mountain goat as she walked with the firewood on her unclad shoulders.

The tree, Izmel, the girl, firewood, and the smoke – not a being could he see around in the land north of Chechua. The sky wide high, his shaft on his right hand, and a woven bag inside which there was food and his magnets, where there was not a being except a tree, beneath which he watched the scantily clad breasts hovering above the skin of mountain goat, walking towards the house upon which there was smoke as grey as the a cloudy dusk of winters. His adolescent Ta would push him to the brink of desire, which Izmel withheld for the sake of his fear. Something in his inner self said, Izmel you are thin and withered from travel, if you approach her now you would perish from the folly of your own desire. It would be strange for Siempre to whisper that, because Siempre was Ta – impatient by its own nature – he thus wondered at his duality that had led him to cast Siempre on that fateful dawn. He sat instead under the tree and watched her walk to the house upon which there was smoke as grey as a cloudy dusk of winter, wondering if he could ever approach her, filling the void of his lost pole.

As he rested under the tree, he saw an old man approaching from the house. His name was nameless, for he was too old to remember his name. He was the father of Zerene, the girl who carried firewood. Thus, Izmel called him Abu Zerene (which in Chechuan means, father of Zerene). Abu Zerene, flickering an eye like a candle in the wind about to be exhausted from the perils of his life, looked at the fearful dark eyes of Izmel and said, you look strong young man, for one day you will be like me. Izmel looked at Abu Zerene's withering hand, the wrinkles on his face and wondered about life, death and purpose. Abu Zerene with the comfort of his hand held Izmel's shoulder. His fragile strength brought great comfort to Izmel, a warmth that reminded him of his Pious father.

Izmel, hungry for truth and desire under the shade of the tree, asked Abu Zerene, "why do people get old? A few years ago, when the sun and the moon were still moving around the horizon, when the day could still be distinguishable from night, I had my little Siempre as a dear friend. Now, the sun and the moon have taken many more rounds above us, I have lost my little Siempre, yet the time hasn't stopped, and I saw your daughter. The Ta inside me looked at her beauty, saw the fine hair of her adolescent beauty brushing her shoulders, and craved for her. My Ta wished her to be next to me, so I would find the lost pole of my lost magnet, is she the magnet or the pole?"

The old man, bewildered with Izmel's question, looked at the sky for a while. He wondered who this young man was, who talks in a language alien to the land of Magua, talks about his own daughter, about Ta, Sun and Moon, and magnets and poles. The old man, with the wisdom of his age, said to Izmel,

"you need to find those answers by yourself"

He had initially wished to invite Izmel to his house, but did not anymore.

"You need to move further north where darkness is longer than light, and light is longer than darkness."

Izmel, exhausted by his journey, said, "my body is exhausted; I cannot travel further. I can work for you, help you carry the firewood, carry water with the strength of my youth if you could give me some bread to eat".

Abu Zerene, lost in his compassion for Izmel, agreed to let him in for a week, and said, "you can eat from the blood of my livestock, but you shall not eat from the blood of my soul". Izmel knew what he meant. The land of Magua was full of mystery, and so was the house of Zerene.

As Izmel approached the house of Zerene, he saw piles of books on every corner of the house. He asked Abu Zerene, "whose books are these?" Abu Zerene said, "these are Zerene's books – she reads all night and day, her knowledge encompasses the rooves of this house".

Zerene, having found the anecdote at the end of an age-old gospel, "for every female who makes herself male will enter the kingdom of Heaven", pursued to be a male to become a living spirit. Izmel's curiosity for Zerene flared up so much that he couldn't stand still for a while. His Ta would push him to corners of the house, to get a glimpse of the mystery of Zerene, of the breasts hovering above the skin of mountain goat. He took his shirts off and ran out to find the firewood, in the hope that Zerene will be around. His little Siempre was dead, but Ta was alive, the seed grown into adulthood.

"Zerene", he called from the distance. Zerene looked at Izmel and smiled. He said, "the firewood is taken home to be burnt, what do you have to offer me?" Zerene looked with wonderment at Izmel's question, a language alien to the land of Magua. Zerene, never touched by a man in her life, said "I have ashes in my soul, you cannot burn it anymore". Izmel was as overjoyed as if he had finally found a tribe he could talk to. He wanted to touch her, smell her ashes, and see what the melancholy of life means. As he approached closer to her, Zerene reminded him – "you shall quench your thirst in the blood of the livestock of my father, not the blood of his soul". As Ta subsided with her sharp words, Izmel said, "you are a tree in the land of Magua. I am not allowed to approach you, lest I be thrown out of here. Yet, the Ta inside me persuaded me to taste the fruit in your ashes. By every crawling creature in the land of Magua, I say I shall not step my foot closer to you".

The sky was getting darker, as the dense cloud above wanted to gush its load down to the barren land of Magua. It happens once in every six full moons, that the rain quenches the thirst in the dead soil of Magua. Izmel and Zerene rushed to the house, with loads of firewood on their back. Rain started drizzling down, running through the bare chest of Izmel. Zerene's hair was soaked, letting the drips of rain brush over her dusty shoulders and onto her bosoms hovering above the thirsty skin of the mountain goat. The fire of Ta was quenched by the droplets of rain and Izmel shivered in the coldness. The sheer beauty of Zerene no more attracted Izmel - Izmel thought, "where there is no Ta there is true love".

As Izmel approached the house, Abu Zerene stood with a stick under his feeble hand on the door of his house. His grey hair and silver beard were wet, and his sunken eyes were cooled from the heat of Magua. Izmel threw the stack of firewood on the doorstep and said, "Abu Zerene, I speak the language of your daughter, and I find you with a stick that I had cast away in my childhood."

Abu Zerene again looked at wonderment at Izmel's wisdom and said, "if you fulfill four years in the land of Magua, feed the livestock and take care of my household my blood, Zerene, the blood of my soul, is yours". Abu Zerene continued, "you may not touch her by any means – these four years are an interim for you to fulfil. For if you pass the test, the fruit is yours".

Izmel was astonished to hear this offer. His desire to have Zerene was so great that he succumbed to the old man's deal. Ga wanted a pair to nourish the soul while Ta wanted the pair for its own passion. Izmel stood between Ta and Ga, agreed to the deal and took an oath on the doorsteps of Abu Zerene's house. Rain stopped pouring and clouds cleared, sun was bright at the horizon and livestock rushed back to feed its blood. Zerene walked away bashfully to her chamber with dreams of Izmel in her heart. It was another day at the land of Magua, the land little north of Chechua.

Izmel stepped through the doorstep of Abu Zerene's house, wondering about what he had just vowed. His tender adolescence caused him to think about his mother, father and every little being of his home in Chechua. His eyes were filled for fear of his four years of bondage. He trusted Abu Zerene for his kindness, yet the shackles of commitment were bothering his free spirit. He went to his courtyard and lied down on the comfort of the clayed floor. The earth cooled him as he looked through the window as the smell of earth from the dampness of rain was fading away.

Izmel closed his eyes. He had a new roof, and the adulthood of commitment seemed to be falling from the sky.

As he fell asleep, Ga was appearing in his dreams bringing a great sense of responsibility towards his pair. His pair was in the chamber a few yards away and Izmel felt the first sense of the responsibility of manhood on his chest. It was heavy, but it felt good. It was the heaviness of responsibility, maturity and masculinity – every woman seeks it – an unseen force giving a great sense of security, a secret every man carries through the times of his silence and pride.

As he woke up from sleep with a heavy chest, he gazed at the roof of Abu Zerene's house, at the hay Abu Zerene had covered with his feeble hands. Izmel felt the heaviness of Abu Zerene's chest, of his pious father's chest, of every manhood who strives to protect their pairs from crawling beings. Thus, a man's skin is covered with hair, protecting him from the rays of sun. A woman's skin is laid bare for the roof above her shields her from the toil. Izmel wondered at this wonderful creation, how perfectly man and woman are designed, each complementing one another like the poles of the magnet which are bound to come together.

Zerene in her chamber felt the heaviness of Izmel's chest that was radiating through the house upon which there was smoke as grey as a cloudy dusk of winters. Her bare bosoms expanded over the skin of mountain goat, seeking the heaviness of Izmel's chest, to feel the comfort of his masculine hair. Yet her feminine morality stuck her to the ground, and she gripped her hay filled pillow like the claws of a leopard, falling asleep to the breeze of Magua.

Her dream was that of a mustard seed, lit behind by a brilliant light. The seed approached her, growing larger and larger until it filled the light with blinding darkness. Thus, there was darkness, a darkness spread from a tiny mustard seed over a brilliant light.

As she woke up from the sleep, she wondered at the seed, her large dark eyes gazing at the roof unable to shiver from the fear, her long eyelids so heavy that she could not blink for a while. She wondered, what is this anxiety that strikes me? What wrong have I done? She woke up to find Millie, her cat, next to her brushing her black fur next to her skin. When she sought to take comfort in Millie, Millie ran away like she always did.

Chapter 4

Branches – The limits are unlimited

At about the time when the sun was about to set, the book man arrived. Zerene, upon hearing the sound of his horsecar, got excited and hopped away from her bed – the mustard seed has gone to oblivion for her passion to seek was far stronger. She ran towards the front door and asked, "what news have you bought O' bookman"?

Munger, the bookman said "I travelled to the north for about six months. I met two tribes – one from the west and one from the far east. They crossed the oceans to the Northern land for the northern land was filled with sins and avarice".

Zerene with all curiosity asked, "Munger the bookman, have you really seen the crowd and might of the Northern land? No one from the land of Magua has ever been to the Northern land! How did you get there? Did the people near the great canal not stop you? How did you cross the wall? And how did you get back"?

Izmel overheard these questions sat next to Zerene in the corridor. It was the first time Izmel heard of the Northern land.

Munger, overwhelmed by Zerene's questions said, "getting to the Northern land was hard and heavy. When I was close to the grand canal, I met someone who had managed to go to the Northern land. He said, "the Northern land has got a new emperor, his face is orange and he likes anyone with an orange face". So, I painted myself orange and walked further towards the north. I found large machines building huge walls, as tall as the mountains of the south".

Izmel interrupted, "what are machines?"

Munger, annoyed with Izmel's question asked Zerene, "who is this boy?" As Zerene blushed, Izmel felt as if someone has pricked on his pumped-up masculine chest with a sharp needle – his illusion of a fully grown up man was thwarted as Munger called him a boy. Zerene, seeing Izmel's embarrassing smile said to Munger, this is Izmel from the land of Chechua. He is helping my father to feed the livestock and carry the woods. Izmel, further belittled, for he believed he to be the heir of Abu Zerene's household, said to himself, "I better leave this house and be my own than live like a slave".

Munger said, "okay, young man, machines are alive, they eat and drink, but they are not animals. They are made out of iron. They drink murky liquid to feed themselves. Unlike the horses, they do not feed themselves – humans should pour the liquid to their throats. They gulp as much as you pour, and never say stop. But as dumb as it sounds machines have great strength. They can vanish a mountain, they can fly beyond the sky and they are a hundred times faster than horses."

Izmel, curious, asked "do machines smile?"

Zerene, astonished by Izmel's question, thought to herself, "I have read so many books about machines, but I have never asked this to myself".

Munger said, "machines do not smile or cry – they obey what their masters say. They are like horses, but if you hit a horse too hard it may kick you back, if you try to kill a horse it will run away, but machines won't. If you kick a machine, your foot will be hurt, but the machine will not say a thing."

Izmel, unconvinced with this answer, asked "if machines cannot cry or laugh, why do humans use them"?

Zerene got excited and said, "I can answer this! Izmel, humans do not care if the horses smile, all they care is if the horse makes them smile. When the bloody preachers with crosses visited our land, they came here with horses. Our good old kings did not care if horses smiled or cried, all they cared was if the horses made them smile. But then the thunder struck our land and we were lost to the jungles."

Munger said, "well said Zerene. In the land of Northern land there are big machines and small machines. There are machines to go from land to land, there are machines upon which they fly, there are machines they hold in their hands – they think they can make them smile and happy, but the more machines they have the more they need."

Abu Zerene, overhearing this discussion from his chamber coughed hard and said, "we were happy walking, then we wanted canoes, and the bloody preachers with crosses bought wheels and horses, are we happier now?"

Everyone had a moment of silence, pondering themselves if they were happy.

Munger broke the silence, and said, "Anyway, I painted myself orange and walked to the...."

Izmel, still pondering about machines, interrupted again "I know a person who molded iron into steel, wired silicon into marvelous lights and sought spirits unknown."

Munger got into deep thought – he knew this young man was not ordinary, but being a shrewd tradesman he was reluctant to show any excitement towards Izmel. He had heard from his travels that there was a man in Chechua who had inordinate abilities to create new things. From his travels to the Northern land, he had little doubt that Izmel was talking about machines, machines in the land of Chechua.

The old man, hearing that the conversation was going nowhere, coughed and said "Lend your ears to the man with more wisdom. Otherwise, you are losing the trade of knowledge." Izmel said, "Abu Zerene, if what you say is true the world will be in silence – no one would want to speak for the fear of losing knowledge".

Izmel was happy to see Zerene grin for his quip.

Trying to ease the situation, Munger asked, "so, folks – what do you want me to speak about, the two tribes, machines, knowledge or travel?" Zerene said, "you always talk about your travel, I know enough about machines, and I have read a lot for my age, tell me about the two tribes" Izmel said, "I know little about everything, so my ears are all open".

Munger looked at Izmel and said, "you will not understand the tale of two tribes unless you know about knowledge. So, let me talk about knowledge and will let you know about the two tribes I met in the Northern land. But promise not to ask me any questions until the sun sets tonight".

Izmel agreed, and Munger continued.

"Knowledge is hidden until you know it. Knowledge has always been there; it is here, and it is in the Northern land. The essence of the knowledge of making machines is in the universe, but we live in oblivion about machines until it is revealed to us. When it is revealed to a man, he may use it or forget it. Millions of knowledge is lost that way, never trying, never used by anyone. If all the knowledge revealed to mankind was not forgotten and instead was used, we would have seen marvels we could not even imagine.

When I went to the Northern land, I thought the machines were spirits or that I was dead and in a different world. I could not believe that I was seeing machines fly, and people talking to far away distances through machines. I climbed up the tree when I saw a four-wheel machine at the distance, for I was afraid the spirit would devour me. But, when I knew that it was knowledge, everything became normal to me. I realized that this is knowledge that is hidden in the land of Chechua, in the land of Magua and wherever I have traveled. But the people of the Northern land used it when it was revealed to them. I saw everyone working hard for their own good, people with knowledge being rewarded for what they had revealed. Thus, I saw knowledge flying with its wings high and wide.

I saw the people in the Northern land had perfected the art of acquiring knowledge and selling it. If I bring a four wheeled machine from the Northern land, which runs ten times faster than a horse and can carry a hundred times the load of a horse, I bet not a man in the land of Magua will trade their ten dear horses to the four-wheeled-machine. But, in the Northern land, the tradesmen have perfected the art of mind – they will sell the machine with so much elegance that it becomes a dream for every Northern man to buy it even though he would never have to carry the load of hundred horses. Thus, everyone in the Northern land has giant machines, some of them even loading machines in their yards for no other reasons but to show to their neighbors.

In the Northern land, I went to a shop where they sold a cooked meatloaf in between bread. People were crowding to eat it, they all talked how good it was. I wondered why nobody in Magua thought about it. We have meat and bread here; all we need is to put the meat between the bread and add some cucumbers and peppers. I thought I could open a shop selling cooked meat in between bread with some cucumbers and I can become rich. But when I came back and said to my wife about the idea I stole from the Northern land, she laughed at me. She said, "you can borrow the necklace of your other wife to start the shop, not mine!" So, I went to my other wife and told about my idea. So, on until I went to my tenth wife, and when she laughed, I thought I should give up my idea. I realized same knowledge I had learnt doesn't work everywhere. For a knowledge to work it may require many other knowledges to work too. In the land of Magua, the other knowledges were missing to make my stolen idea work.

I met a fat lady in that shop of the Northern land, and I thought she must be very rich. She was very fat, dark skinned and had ten kids around her. She ordered the meat with two breads for all of them, and a very dark and sweet drink for all of them including a large mug for herself. I was feeling very happy that I actually met a very rich woman. I wondered if the emperor with the orange face liked only people with orange faces, why the woman with the dark face was so rich. So, I decided to talk to her.

I said, "hello madam. I am honored to meet you; I am very glad that I could find someone like you with ten kids". She looked at me with caution, as if I was going to kill her. I said, "my face is only painted orange because I wanted to visit this empire. I am a traveler, coming from the land of Magua, a little north to the land of Chechua". She was oblivious, she looked at me as if no land existed outside the Northern land. I thought I could marry her and live a happy life with all her wealth.

I said, "you look beautiful madam. Are you married"? She said, "no I am not married. My husband left me a year ago". I wondered why her husband would have left such a beautiful dark fat lady. I said, "I am sorry to hear that madam. Maybe I can help you, madam. I have a large bookstore in the land of Magua, I have ten wives and I will be happy to invite you to marry me". She looked at me in surprise, as if I had done something wrong. She said, "I am sorry sir, I might be poor, fat and homeless, I might be having ten kids, but I don't want no man having ten wives". It took me a while to decipher her logic, and I said, "yes madam, don't feel sorry, I know you don't want no man having no ten wives – for your beauty you definitely deserve a man with many more wives". She said, "are you crazy?", and left out of my sight with all her beautiful fat black little kids.

I wondered at her sarcasm. Her language was all mixed up. I did not know if she was actually homeless or was sarcastic because she did not like me. So, I decided to follow her. As she was walking with her ten kids, I found her begging from a stranger. I wondered how she could be so fat being so poor. The Northern land is strange. In the land of Magua, when poor men tie a sack of sand to his belly not to feel the hunger and the rich man ties up a rope to not let his belly fall, in the Northern land it is the opposite. Every rich man in the Northern land ties a piece of cloth to their neck like the shackles of a slave in the land of

Magua, even in the hottest of the Northern summer – a very interesting land indeed."

Everyone started laughing, and the old man laughed so much hearing this that he could not stop coughing. Zerene got worried and went inside the house to help the old man relieve his cough.

When Zerene left, Izmel whispered to Munger. "My pious father was well off, and my mother took good care of me, but I left my home in the land of Chechua to find the truth about life and the purpose of our existence. As hard it is for me to believe in your story, I want to visit the Northern land and experience it for myself – perhaps I may find answers to my questions there. I have vowed a four years contract here, but I need to escape." Munger, hearing his eagerness, said "Izmel I will let you travel to the Northern land, if you..."

Munger seeing Zerene walking back abruptly changed the topic, and said "yes, the emperor with the orange face had a wide support from the orange faced deprived, but like all other strange stories in the Northern land he was among the rich and lived in a Golden mansion. One would wonder why the poor would be so found of a man who has always been fed by golden spoon."

Izmel nodded with a giggle looking at Munger's clever eyes.

Zerene said, "maybe he was like the prince from the east who left his palace to the woods in the land of elephants."

Munger thought for a while and said, "no that cannot be the case because the prince from the east meditated for the rest of his life and never sought the golden spoon again. The emperor with the orange face has two wide palaces; one painted white and the other painted with fine gold."

The old man said from inside the chamber, "there is a saying in the land of Magua, the eyes seek what the heart yearns."

Munger said, "yes that is a good proposition. Maybe the poor yearned for everything the rich Emperor had, so the poor thought the rich Emperor would make them rich."

Zerene said, "well if that is the case then why do the rich men in the Northern land not support the orange emperor? – the rich always want to be richer."

Munger said, "that is a good question Zerene. For you to know the answer you need to know certain truths about being rich."

"The sun rises and sets at the same time everywhere in the land of Magua. Yet, we find some people wealthy enough to afford horses and sheep, while others toil the soil all day long to get a piece of food. Why is it so? Why do some have more than the rest?

Nature is not still; it changes many times and the change changes many times. So, in a day of time if the rich has a quarter of time to spare, he can use that quarter of time to make many more free quarters of time. Meanwhile, the poor man toiling all day has no time to spare and can create no extra quarters of time. Instead the man who he toils for earns all the quarters of time. Thus, the change of change acts in the favor of who has time to spare.

Many such quarters of time got accumulated in the Northern land, and the whole land became so rich that there are decades of time free for every person. Thus, the poorest man in the Northern land will be richer than the richest man in the land of Magua, for the poorest man in the Northern land has more quarters of time than the richest man in the land of Magua.

The rich men in the Northern land have accumulated decades of quarters of time, while the poor men in the Northern land have only a few months of quarters of time, often donated by the mercy of the orange government. So, the rich men and women of the Northern land have so many quarters of time to spare that they have a lot of time to think. They see the poor men and women working hard driving their machines, cooking food and teaching their children. Thus, they think the nature is unfair to make some have more quarters of time than the others. They live a life of guilt, and the only way they can feel good is to think that the poor men and women should have everything that they have. So, the rich men of the Northern land do not like the Orange man who says that there should be nothing free in the Northern land and everyone has to work hard to accumulate their own quarters of time."

Izmel was so tempted to question Munger's logic, but the sun was still further away from the horizon.

Zerene asked, "so Munger the bookman, why on earth do the poor men of the Northern land support the Orange emperor, when he says nothing is free."

Munger got annoyed and said, "Zerene you are asking the same question again! We all agreed earlier with your father that the eyes seek what the heart yearns. The heart of the poor yearns to be rich, not the quarters of time. Even if they have a quarter of time on their hand, they will not use it to make two quarters of the time. They will spend all the quarters of time to make them feel that they are rich. The Orange emperor knows this, and he does not give anything for free, he only promises that everyone will be rich one day. He continues to fly in his golden machine so that the poor men of the Northern land will look high and dream to be like the Orange man someday."

The sun was about to set, and Izmel became totally restless. Everyone could see Izmel's restlessness, and they waited for him to speak, to ask a profound question no one has ever thought. As soon as the tip of the sun touched the barren mountains of the land of Magua, Izmel asked, "do we have anything to eat? I am hungry."

Upon which everyone laughed, and the old man from inside said, "the mouth seeks what the stomach yearns."

Chapter 5
Green Branch – The first tribe

As Zerene went in to prepare food, Munger whispered to Izmel, "I will show you the way to the Northern land if you would show me the man who molded iron into steel and wired silicon into marvelous lights." Izmel nodded his head side to side (in the land of Chechua, nodding head from side to side – from one shoulder to other – is to show affirmation) and walked outside to collect wood for the night fire.

After everyone had food, they sat around the night fire which Izmel had prepared in front of the house. Zerene got a thick blanket to cover Abu Zerene and she sat next to him. Abu Zerene said to Munger, "so tell us the story of the two tribes".

Munger said, "I will tell you the story of the first tribe tonight for it is more fitting for me to tell the story of the second tribe when the sun is at its horizon either at the dawn or at the dusk."

"The first tribe I met was at the southern end of the Northern land. I met the tribe where the cactus grew as large as the mountains, where the stars were seen as clear as crystals. Before I tell you the story of the first tribe, I want to warn you this. If you happen to learn this news, and you don't obey the news, great calamity will touch you. But, if you happen to learn this news and obey it you will have everlasting happiness".

Izmel said to himself, "what greater calamity can touch me? I have left my house, abandoned my parents and lost my little Siempre".

Abu Zerene, wise enough for his age, stood up and told Zerene to go inside the house with him. Hearing this, Zerene pleaded, "I am a woman. Someday I may have to bear the burden of my seed, and I will have to go through great pain. If I listen, perhaps I will be saved from the perils of my womanhood".

Abu Zerene, hearing her folly said "you do not know what you speak. Get inside the house, for I do not want you to fall for the perils of misfortunes".

Zerene, having no choice, walked inside the house with the old man.

Munger asked Izmel, "what about you Izmel, are you ready to hear the story of the first tribe?"

Izmel again nodded from side to side.

Munger continued, "whoever listens to this let them know that they are hearing the truth about the first tribe. Izmel, you have indeed passed the first test, and you have willingly agreed to listen to the truth of the first tribe. Congratulations!"

Izmel opened his mouth in wonderment on what he had agreed upon.

Munger said, "In the southern land of the Northern land, where the cactus grows as tall as the mountains and the stars were seen to be as clear as crystals, I met the first tribe. Every one of them had a book in their hand which they carried with great care.

Me being a bookman, wondered what the book was. So, I told the first man I met that I am Munger the bookman coming from Magua, and I have colored myself in orange to walk past the wall – in fact, my skin like your skin is brown in color. He was happy to hear that and asked me if I have ever heard about the book in his hand. I said, no, so he took me with him to a place whose four green walls were equal in size, and whose roof resembled the shell of an egg.

I went inside and he gave me the copy of the book, then he left. I was happy to get the book without having to pay him anything, not even a piece of gold, let alone the expensive spices I carried with me. So, I decided to read the book inside the room under the roof of an eggshell.

The book had unique symbols in front of some chapters, some chapters were long while others were short. Each chapter began in the name of God, except the ninth one. I was astonished at the symbols, and the language resembling that of those from the east of Chechua. I read word by word, many of the verses were clear as the sky of the southern land of the Northern land, and some of the verses were obscured like the eggshell roof that covered me.

The book was warning and hope, guidance and mercy. As I read the book, I was agonized with fear of everything I had done in the past. The idols, spirits, sacrifices and everything we do in the land of Chechua and Magua was punishable by the God of the book. The supreme God created the sun, moon, animals, spirits, air, water, me, you and everything known and unknown. I have never heard of this supreme God before except from the brutal Preachers with crosses who destroyed our tribes, but the God of

Preachers were three, the God of this book is one – the one God, the supreme God who controls everything in this universe. The book ordains everyone to worship the supreme God alone, and no one else. Worshiping any spirits or men would lead to an abominable place called hell, where one shall burn forever.

So, I waited with fear all night, I could not eat or drink for three days. After three days while still sitting out of fear and wonderment in the room under the roof of an eggshell, I saw the man with the brown skin again. He kissed my cheek like my wife would kiss the son of my mother. I said, "O' man with the color of my skin, I cannot sleep or eat, everything we are doing in the land of Chechua and Magua seems wrong. I hope your supreme God does not punish us."

So, he smiled at me and said, "now you know!" and he gave me another book. This time I offered him a few gold coins in exchange for the book, and he said, "if all the trees in the planet were pens and oceans were ink, supplied with seven more oceans, the words of God will not run out". Thus, the man with the brown skin left in peace. His smile was so powerful that I couldn't help thinking of all the sadness I had gone through during my life. He truly seemed to have found contentment in his life. I left the room under the roof of an eggshell to the outskirts of the city. While leaving the beautiful building, I turned back to read what was written above the front door – it said, "Happiness is Submission to God alone".

As I kept walking towards a mountain, I found a giant cactus. So, I decided to read the new book under one of the giant cacti, and it began with "we have given you the seven pairs" – fourteen strange signs in front of twenty-nine chapters. And then it said, "over it is nineteen".

The book counted the symbols on each chapter, intertwined with each other to form a web of nineteen – so tightly holding the words of the book that if one word is changed, the web will fall apart. For many hundred years, the book was hidden under the strange symbols. Now, it has come to light the meaning of these strange symbols in the land where cactus grows as tall as the mountains, where the stars were as clear as crystals. Someday, when the stars will fall apart and the mountains will be blown out, humans will start lamenting about how they missed this profound miracle. Izmel, thus you have fulfilled the covenant. You have now known"!

Izmel, upon hearing this story, was utterly amazed. Izmel said, "Munger the bookman, all my life I was waiting to find a tribe like the first tribe. I held tight to the stick for the love of the man who crossed the sea, but Siempre blew his spirits on me to cast away the stick. I have heard the truth that was hidden in the gospels that Preachers with crosses brought to us. The Preachers with crosses worshiped the man who spoke the words – what a terrible sin in light of the wisdom of the first tribe". Izmel continued, "I submit to the God of the first tribe, the God of the man who crossed the sea and the God of the man who spoke the words".

Munger having heard this said, "you have known and believed but the test shall come upon which you must not fail. The two paths are clear, and you have chosen the difficult path."

When he heard this, Izmel asked, "Munger the bookman, what are the two paths and how do I distinguish them? What shall I do to make sure that I won't burn in agony under the fire of hell"?

Munger said, "the two paths are clear as light and darkness. The easy path, which humans by large lead themselves along with the spirits who follow the king of chaos to the everlasting hell is short-term. The easy path craves for near not the distance. Anything you do to satisfy the desire of now is the easy path which will lead to great difficulty. Ask yourself before you drink and eat, crave for woman or wealth, ask yourself is it for now or distance.

The path that is difficult is the one which leads to benefits in the distance. There might be a bit of a pain at the present, but the reward is great. Ask yourself before you drink and eat, crave for woman or wealth, ask yourself is it for now or distance."

Hearing this, Izmel trembled with fear, fell down to his knees and asked the supreme God for pardon. Izmel said, "Munger the bookman, I have thought of my temporary lust and greed, I desired Zerene as I had desired Siempre. I was thinking only of now, which lead to grief upon grief. But when I agreed to Abu Zerene to stay here for four years in exchange for my freedom, I felt the hardship, but it bought inner peace in me. I felt I had a purpose, that my energy was to be spent for something good. When I carry the wood to the house, I feel the same. But when I crave for the sensual pleasures of Zerene, it brings grief upon grief".

Munger said, "very well said Izmel, the supreme God promises eternal peace in Heavens to those who pass the test, but the reward starts from here. You have experienced the pain and bliss; many people have experienced the pain and bliss. Izmel, think for the distance, work for the distance, choose the difficult path and you shall be happy".

The firewood exhausted, Izmel and Munger fell prostrated to the Creator and the night was out.

Thus, was the story of the first tribe, the tribe which purifies by the mercy of the supreme God.

Chapter 6
Brown branch – The second tribe

As Izmel woke up the next day at the dawn, he saw Munger sitting under a tree whose roots fell from the shoots of the branches. Munger was still as a rock, with his eyes closed. As Izmel went closer, Munger smiled with tears in his eyes. Seeing this, Zerene and Abu Zerene came closer and sat next to Munger. And Munger said,

"The sun is in the horizon and I shall tell you the story of the second tribe". Abu Zerene interrupted, "hold on Munger the bookman. I have never been harsh with you nor have I treated you unfairly. In the darkness of yesterday, you told us the news of the first tribe with the condition that shook the house of Magua. Now, you are telling the story of the second tribe and I am afraid for the love of my only daughter Zerene".

Munger said, "do not worry O' father of Zerene. You shall not fear about the story of the second tribe for I am afraid the calamity might have already touched you for ignoring the story of the first tribe."

Abu Zerene became furious upon hearing this; his eyes became red and his hands shook more than usual. The stick he carried almost broke from the anger gushing through his veins. Abu Zerene said "you son of the concubine, I made you rich buying your books for the love of my only daughter, and now you betrayed my soul with the stories from the Northern land. I shall throw you to the spirits of Chechua if you utter anything more in the house of Magua."

Munger, smiling, said to Abu Zerene. "I am no more afraid of the spirits of Chechua, for I have learnt about the one who created those spirits. I have surrendered to the God of the worlds, and my fear is only my Lord's anger."

Hearing this, Abu Zerene started to cough. His voice subsided and he sat under the tree whose roots fell from the shoots of the branches. While Zerene ran to house to get some water, Munger said,

"O' Abu Zerene take a moment to observe your breath. It comes and goes every moment; thou have no control whatsoever on it. It started when you were born, and it continues until you die. Like birds that fly and animals that walk the earth we all breath willingly or unwillingly, and hardly do we ever notice the breath. The first tribe thanked the supreme God for the breath, the second tribe merely observes the breath. Both actions lead to one thing – awareness of our senses".

Abu Zerene, still breathing heavily, moved his hand, asking Munger to continue.

Munger continued, "I met the second tribe in the northern land of the Northern land, where they seclude themselves for the fear of life. When I met the first man, I asked "O' man with orange robe, what pursuit do you have in your life"? And the man said, "to die so that I shall not be born again".

I asked myself what do they even mean? When we die and becomes dust and bones, you will be born either for the everlasting peace or the agony of the hell. He said, "observe your breath and you shall know".

So, I wiped my face on my robe and pretended to be one among them. I said, "O' man with the orange robe – now, I am one among you, teach me how to observe breath". He took me to the mountains of the northern land of the Northern land and said, "you shall observe your breath from dawn to dusk for three days and you shall vow to not to talk to anyone for three days. You shall not kill any being that lives on earth, and you shall eat from the alms of another soul".

Thus, I left to the mountains of the northern land of the Northern land observing my breath every foot I took. I climbed the mountains, and the breath went faster, and when I took rest at dusk the breath went slower.

I was tired and exhausted as I climbed up the mountain, I was hungry, and I could not see a single soul from who I can ask food for. I was tempted to eat the meat and fruits of the mountains, but I could not for I was not allowed to eat anything from my pride. When I was anxious from not having food, my breath went faster and then it was normal again after a while. Then I found a tree with berries as large as coconuts, and I begged the tree for some berries (I wasn't allowed to talk, so I would fold my hands and cry). Then I would see the tree dropping the fruit on the soil, upon which I would eat them. When my stomach was full, I would feel great happiness, and my breath would be so slow that I would fear I was going to die. I realized that fast breath is temporary, and so is slow breath. Eventually both fast and slow breath will lead to a normal breath, syncing itself with the nature. On the third day on the mountain, I would hear every leaf fall down from the wind, and I would see every shooting star in the sky.

So, having felt this great accomplishment I returned down to the man with the orange robe and said, "for three days I have observed my breath and fulfilled the vow of my silence". He smiled at me and said, "now go to the cave and observe yourself from the tip of your head to the tip of your foot. You shall do this for seven days and you shall not think anything else nor shall you blame yourself nor shall you crave yourself, and you shall vow again not to talk to anyone".

I said to myself, "why am I doing this? Maybe I should just return to the land of Magua. Maybe these men with orange robes are crazy". But, having already spent three days observing my breath and sharpening my mind, I decided to go to the cave.

The cave was dark, and I could count the days from the glimpses of light through the cracks in the rock. I took some berries and fruits with me, and water to drink from the nearby spring.

I sat in the cave with my eyes closed. My mind was so sharp that I could hear every crawling being, every drop of water that would fall from the precipice. I then started to observe myself from the tip of my head to the tip of my foot.

On the first day of the seven days, there was great pain. No matter how I sat, the pain would come – my mind was so sharp that the pain of one time would feel like the pain of ten times. Being a bookman, I used to sit and read for long hours and I would never feel the pain. But in the cave when I was observing with the sharpness of my mind, every moment would feel like my bones were cracking and my back was breaking. I would observe the pain, but I was not allowed to blame myself. So, I would just observe the pain.

On the second and third day of the seven days, the pain continued, but I realized pain comes in waves. Like the fast and slow breath, there are longer and shorter pains. But the pain was temporary too, and just like fast and slow breaths, it arises and passes away.

On the fourth day of seven days, I realized that the pain exists, but my mind was strong enough to bear the pain. I would no longer cry but sit still for long hours observing the pain as it arises and passes away.

On the fifth day of seven days, I would observe the waves of breath and pain, and I would feel them to be tiny vibrations, so tiny in time that I do not know if they were timeless. The vibration in pain and breath continued. I started observing those vibrations, and I would feel great pleasure. The more I felt the vibration, the more I wanted it. I would observe the pleasure, but I was not allowed to crave myself. Thus, I merely noticed the pleasant vibrations arising and passing away.

On the sixth day of seven days, I felt the pain again, and I thought the vibration I had achieved was lost. I thought I had done something wrong, and that I would no longer feel the pleasant vibration. I spent the first half of the sixth day of the seven days in disappointment. I felt so disappointed that I thought of leaving. But in the second half of the sixth day of seven days, the pain subsided, and I could feel the vibration again. The cycle of the grossness of pain and subtleness of vibration continued for the rest of the day, until I realized that pain and pleasure are part of life and being disappointed is a folly.

Thus, came the seventh day of the seven days, and I continued to observe the tiny vibrations. These tiny vibrations felt the same, there was no pain or pleasure. I realized pain and pleasures are just illusions, while the reality is the tiny vibrations which are agnostic to what mind interprets from them. I realized both pain and pleasure are the same at their core – they are all tiny particles of vibrations. Having felt this, I felt great compassion for the human beings who are suffering from the illusion of pain and pleasure. So, I decided to send my compassion for everyone else and I could feel the smile on my face.

I left the cave with the smile and smiled at the man with the orange robe. He smiled at me back. I did not utter a word to him, nor did he utter a word to me. Thus, I left the northern land of the Northern land with a smile, and thus was the story of the second tribe. This story is like the time of this dawn, when the time is neither at the night nor at the day but something in between."

Once Munger had finished talking, Abu Zerene, Izmel and Zerene closed their eyes to see if they could feel their vibrations. Upon witnessing this Munger felt very happy. Zerene opened her eyes and said, this is the middle path that I read from the book of the East. Munger smiled, and he dispersed with Izmel for his morning worship according to the laws of the first tribe.

Chapter 7

The fruit – The bait of illusion

It was time for Munger to bid farewell. Little did Abu Zerene know that Munger had a secret deal with Izmel.

Abu Zerene, seeing Munger pack his books and cloths went near him and said,

"I apologize for what I said, in fact I must thank you for the lessons you have given to the house of Magua."

Munger came closer to Abu Zerene and said, "you do not have to apologize O' father of Zerene - you gave me an opportunity to explain the story of the second tribe".

Abu Zerene said, "I was too afraid to learn the story of the first tribe, for the veil was in front of me. Now, I have cast aside my veil, so please tell me the story of the first tribe". Munger thus sat next to Abu Zerene, and told the story of the first tribe - about the man with the brown skin, the two books, the room under the roof of an eggshell, the cactus which grew as large as the mountains, the hidden miracle, the number nineteen and the truth.

After Munger had finished, Abu Zerene cast aside every deity of Chechua and fell down on his knees submitting himself to the God of the universes.

As Munger was about to leave, Zerene and Izmel went near him to bid farewell. Izmel walked with Munger to the gate of Magua and told him the way to Siempre's house in Chechua.

Munger said, "on the sixth day of the seventh month, you shall stand in the gates of Chechua and I shall, by the will of God, show you the path to the Northern land".

Both nodded their heads side to side and departed.

Izmel went home amazed at the wisdom he had learned in the past two days. He thanked God for the immense opportunities he had received from Munger and Abu Zerene. He thought the Ta was dead, and that his Ga had overtaken the Ta. With pride and ease he went down under the tree whose roots fell from its branches and meditated for the rest of the day.

In the morning the next day, as the colorful rooster of Chechua called for the prayer at dawn, Izmel went down for prostration. On his way back from prayer, he saw Zerene through the windows of her courtyard.

Izmel thought to himself, "now my Ga has overtaken Ta, my Siempre has been crunched by the wisdom of the first and second tribe. I am strong as the rocks of the northern land of the Northern land, or maybe even stronger for in the rocks in the cave of the northern land of the Northern land there were cracks through which light shone in. Let me go to the window and see Zerene, for I know I am strong and I wish to test my strength."

As Izmel approached Zerene he felt the Ta arising, and his heart pounded with all its glory. Izmel was conscious of his fear, and could feel his Ta, so he said to himself, "perhaps I am stronger now. I am bold to face my Ta for if I run from Ta how shall I prove that I am strong? If I run from Ta how can I ever pass the test"? So, Izmel slowly approached the window of Zerene's courtyard, his heart pounding and his Ta rising. Through the window that opened to a vastness of light and heaven, he saw Zerene lying bare on the skin of the mountain goat. His eyes were stunned by the beauty of a woman, for Izmel in his adulthood had never seen a woman unclad. He looked at the wonder God had created and saw the curves of her unclad womanhood.

Izmel, hypnotized with the charm of his Ta, went inside the house and sneaked to her courtyard. Beneath the load of books and the roof of the house upon which there was smoke as grey as a cloudy dusk of winters, he saw his desire, Zerene sleeping unclad on the skin of the mountain goat.

Not a thought of the first or second tribe would pass the strength of Ta hypnotizing the mind of this adult man. His chest was pounding, his eyes were fixed on what Izmel saw before him, which was like nothing he had seen before. He did not take a step further, instead his feet took the steps themselves, until he stepped on the skin of the mountain goat on which Zerene slept unclad. His feet were like the claws of a mountain leopard, for they knew they would devour the mountain goat, and with all care they moved not to wake up the slumber of its beloved desire.

He neared to her, smelt the fragrance of womanhood, and made every care of not hurting her for he loved what he desired with all his heart. He tenderly felt her skin, the warmth of his hand feeling her hairless body, moving his hands as though he never wanted to remove them from her.

Upon feeling the callus of Izmel's hands, Zerene woke up with fear in her eyes. She wondered if it was Abu Zerene or Millie, but when she opened her eyes she saw her beloved's eyes, looking at her as if he had never seen a woman. Zerene tried to grab the skin of the mountain goat to cover herself before it was too late. It was late, too late for Izmel in silence had clawed her with his Ta.

Ta pushed him to the brink of his desire, his nose brushing the scent of his desire, his hands caressing the curves of Zerene, with great pride at the coarseness of his manly hands, which gave great comfort to Zerene's feeble womanhood. As the Ta overtook Ga, the books in the courtyard witnessed along with the roof, and they wondered at what they preached, the countless words and wisdoms in the books written were obscured. Zerene did not say a word, for her eyes were subdued at the grace of Izmel.

Finally, when the little Siempre in Izmel arose with all its strength and as he pounded to take a bite on the neck of Zerene, Abu Zerene heard the noise of falling books, of falling wisdom, and opened the door. He yelled, "O' son of Chechua, what have you done? I have given you this house for the respite of your soul. You have broken your vow to not touch the blood of my soul! I trusted you with my only daughter and now this house is no more your house, and my daughter is no more for you"!

Izmel and Zerene, shaken with shame and disgrace grabbed their clothes to cover their shyness. Their bodies were exposed to the brittleness of their souls. Izmel could not utter a word to Abu Zerene, for he knew he had betrayed his soul.

He looked at Zerene with guilt in his eyes, for he thought he had betrayed her soul. He walked away with shame, grabbed his belongings and walked out of the house upon which there was smoke as grey as a cloudy dusk of winters. He cried out loud, "O' Siempre what have you done to me! I meditated and submitted, yet I am weak. I have betrayed the soul of the woman who loved me, and the man who offered me shelter when I was starving".

As he ran away from the house of Abu Zerene, he saw Zerene through the windows of her courtyard. He had sought the seed through the windows, for the fruit was too tempting to resist. He had smelled the fruit, touched the fruit but before even taking a bite, he had run away. He told himself that the fruit clad on the seeds of Zerene was Zerene's. How can it be unlawful to take a bite of the fruit of Zerene, when Zerene owns the fruit? Pondering this, he left the house of Abu Zerene, casting the fruit away from his masculine desire.

Chapter 8

The soil – In the wilderness

It was the first day of the seventh month. There were five more days to go until he met with Munger. For five days of scorching heat, Izmel felt nothing but the pain of his regret. His heart was filled with guilt, his mind was filled with fear and his skin was dry from the heat.

The fruit falls with its beloved seeds from the tree – a few flourishing the seed, while many flourishing the soil.

As fruit falls with its seeds from the tree, there lies the soil waiting for what it could devour, for the soil thinks the fruit will feed it, while the fruit thinks soil will feed its beloved seeds. The soil wins a thousand times – it devours as many fruits as it can, leaving the seeds to the perils of their destiny, but then there is one fruit, one single fruit out of a thousand fruits, who feeds its seeds strong with might. And one of its seeds with all its strength grows, creeping its roots wherever it can, devouring as much soil as possible; thus, that seed grows into a mighty tree, strong and wild devouring the soils where it stood.

That tree grows thousands of seeds, of which some succeed, and many perish. The soil thinks it is always victorious- as thousands of seeds are devoured by it, the tree loses hope until it sees that one seed sneaking its roots into the ground to grow into a magnificent tree devouring thousands of soil.

Izmel walked into the wilderness and saw the gate of Chechua, a tree, tall and strong, a beacon of hope for the birds and crawling beings in the land of Chechua. Izmel thought to himself: I, a mortal man walking with two legs breaths like the birds of the land of Chechua. He sat beneath the tree and ate some fruits that has fallen on the shade. Thus, Izmel implored God saying, "O' God, your mercy encompasses every being. I am guilty for what I did and still you give me fruit to eat and air to breath!"

On the second day of seventh month, he saw a Hoopoe in the tree. The Hoopoe would come close to him then fly away. Izmel looked at the Hoopoe and said, "bird you neither know the words of Chechua nor of Magua, yet you come close to me for the smell of life brings warmth to every living soul". He wished he could be like the king of the east and send the Hoopoe to faraway place so it could meet Zerene and convey his guilt. Every time Izmel approached the Hoopoe, it would fly away. Nature is ruthless, **for as much warmth as a life desires from another life, there is as much fear as a life will find in another.** Izmel called this his first law, as generations away would write it in books and buildings.

Izmel thought for a while about conquering beings by warmth or fear. He remembered the story of Majiki. Majiki was the emperor of Chechua and he conquered every soul in the land to the south of Chechua with fear. Nobody dared to get close to him, or even question him. A fifty of a hundred of the harvest would go to Majiki, no matter if there was drought or abundance. Izmel asked himself how could Majiki conquer the people who didn't even know him?

Having this thought in mind, Izmel had two ways to get closer to the Hoopoe - being warm or being fierce. He implored, "God, I have nothing in my hand to offer this bird to win his warmth. If I am too harsh to him, he will fly away. God, show me a way I can conquer this bird, so that I will have a friend with me in this barren desert".

Thus, Izmel remembered the story of the second tribe, and he thought, "if humans are governed by pleasant and unpleasant sensations, craving for pleasant sensation and averse for unpleasant sensation, so might be birds". So, Izmel thought about the pleasant and unpleasant sensations of the Hoopoe. He found the Hoopoe digging hard in the soil to find its worms, then it flew away with fear when Izmel neared. Thus, Izmel knew the Hoopoe's pleasant and unpleasant sensations: food and fear of getting harmed.

So, Izmel dug hard to find worms. He threw half of the worms to the Hoopoe and ate the other half. Izmel carefully threw each worm closer and closer to him, until finally the Hoopoe was standing on his lap. He had won the heart of the Hoopoe with warmth. He would hug the Hoopoe, kiss the Hoopoe, and love the Hoopoe. Hoopoe, the bird which feared Izmel now craves for Izmel, in his sleep and in his dream. Even when Izmel pushed the Hoopoe away, it flew back to him! What a wonder of nature - the Hoopoe which ran away from Izmel now can't live without him.

And so, Izmel realized that the people of Majiki did not fear Majiki, they feared their own lives. They know if they do not give half of their harvest to Majiki, Majiki would take their lives. Thus, while Majiki, the emperor of fear thought every soul south of Chechua feared him, not a single soul feared him. If they found him alone, they would cut him in pieces and let the holy jaguars feed on his flesh. Majiki, like every arrogant soul, would finally perish from his own ignorance.

Izmel thought perhaps the Hoopoe feared the lack of food, the lack of warmth, the lack of love. Izmel thought again, perhaps the Hoopoe came all the way to his lap for fear of hunger, and not for the love of worms. Izmel further thought, perhaps **fear and craving are one and the same, for in every craving there is a fear.** Izmel called this his second law, as generations away would write it in books and buildings.

Izmel feeling wise, as he has discovered two laws in two days, and thought he had gained enough knowledge to conquer anyone under the stars. So, he dug more worms and left with the Hoopoe to find more food.

Izmel said to himself, "I am walking to the north" and he said, "the sun shall be on my right until the noon passes, and then on my left until the night falls". The Hoopoe followed wherever Izmel walked, and the heat of the desert subsided to the ruthless chill as the sun approached the darkness. Not a tree nor rock, Izmel and the Hoopoe had no place to stay in the barren desert.

The Hoopoe just looking at Izmel at wonder every time he placed his foot towards the light of the north. Izmel felt this burden on his soul, he thought, "if I were alone, I would be responsible for my own death, now if I am lost in the desert what sin did the bird commit to die for me?"

Izmel could hardly breathe, the chill of desert night was so cold that he had to dig himself a hole on the desert soil, and bury himself under the warm sand. As he laid down under the soil, from which he was born, unto which he shall return, he looked high above to the stars, where the sky was crystal clear for the lack of clouds, and he saw the Hoopoe flying, warming itself with the flap of its wings. The night passed and the stars moved above the sky, the Hoopoe flew above Izmel who slept beneath the soil like an ant, not aware of anything above or beneath his mortal body.

As the first rays of sun brushed on his eyelids, Izmel felt the warmth of nature. He said to himself, this is the fourth day of the six days, and I have two more days to get to the gate of Chechua. So, with a loss of hope in finding any food, he started walking back to the south, with the sun to his left until the noon, and to his right until the evening. The Hoopoe, with the love of Izmel, flew behind him with all his love. As the noon passed, and the scorching heat lowered the wings of the Hoopoe, a tiny drop of rain shadowed the eyelids of Izmel. Clouds as dark as the fat lady of the Northern land shadowed the desert for the hopes of every crawling being hiding beneath the sand. Izmel sat on the barren sand with the hope that rain might come to quench his thirst and let him get back to the gate of Chechua.

As the water started gushing forth from the clouds as dark as the fat lady of the Northern land, Izmel opened his mouth to the sky to devour as much water as he could. The Hoopoe raised his beak to the clouds and quenched his thirst as well. The cloud stopped gushing its liquid, the bellies of the crawling beings hiding underneath the soil having been filled with what they desired, and Izmel fell asleep on the dampened sand. The Hoopoe sat on Izmel's shoulder, wondering why he was so in love with a man who neither fed him worms nor gave him warmth.

As time passed by, darkness approached the horizon and Izmel continued sleeping in the dark until the rise of the morn. It was the fifth day of the six days, and Izmel had to get to the gates of Chechua to meet Munger. The clouds were still sitting above him, and the winds had blown the dunes so much that Izmel said, "O' sun, I trusted in you to travel to the south, but now the clouds as dark as the fat lady of Northern land have devoured you, I do not know where I should go."

Clouds, what Izmel craved a day before were now nothing but a burden on his soul.

Izmel said,

"O' cloud, yesterday you looked as beautiful as the dark fat black lady of the Northern land, today you have blinded me with the beauty of your darkness. I wish I had not cursed the heat of the sun, for now my heart is yearning for its light."

As Izmel cried on the floors of sand, the Hoopoe fluttered his wings with increasing frustration. Having been without food for three days, the Hoopoe's patience had been extinguished and it began to fly on its own once more. Izmel, anguished by the treachery of the Hoopoe followed it vehemently. He threw stones from the ground, cursed it all the way under the darkness of the clouds above. Izmel did not care if he was going to the north or the south, his sanity had succumbed to his anger for he couldn't believe that the Hoopoe could disown him. He yelled, "I gave you worms and love, and now you are leaving me alone in this desert cursed by the cloud as dark as the fat lady of the Northern land? I gave you everything, and now you are ignoring me? How can you leave me all alone? Can't you see me crying? I cannot live without your love, please stop flying away! Please take a look at me, perhaps your heart may melt seeing my pain... if you have a heart at all, bird (Izmel did not know it was a Hoopoe). You are truly ungrateful, and I will kill you if I ever get you on my fist. I will love you if you come closer to me and give you whatever you ask me."

The Hoopoe didn't care, no curses or stones could stop him flying, for he knew where he was flying, and he knew what Izmel didn't know.

Izmel sang loud, as loud as he could, so the winds might stop for mercy of his song, and the Hoopoe might get back to Izmel.

He sang,

"A thousand kisses down the shadows I shower on you!
A thousand kisses down the shadows I shower on you!
I shower on you! I shower on you!

I have lost my way! I have lost my way!

Where the world takes down the window, I follow you!
Where the world takes down the window, I follow you!
I follow you! I follow you!

I have lost my way! I have lost my way!"

No song would make the Hoopoe turn back. It flew and flew to what he needed, the worms, the very worms Izmel had forgotten under the tree. After hours of flying he got back to the footsteps of the tree. The Hoopoe ate everything he could leaving not a worm for Izmel.

Izmel, upon seeing the tree, fell in shame. He grabbed the berries to fill his belly. It was the end of the Hoopoe's love with Izmel. No worms or warmth could ever get the Hoopoe back to Izmel's arms, for he was afraid of the stones those arms had thrown.

Chapter 9

On the sixth day of the six days, Izmel saw Munger the bookman. Munger saw Izmel worn and torn under the shades of the tree. He said, "O' Izmel, the young man from Magua, why do you look so tired and withered?" Izmel told him all that had happened, about the meditation, how he got lured to Zerene, why he ran from the house of Abu Zerene, his first law, his second law, how he tamed the Hoopoe, how he lost the Hoopoe, how he got lost in the desert and how he found his way.

Munger hearing this story asked, "where is the bird now?". Izmel was annoyed, because Munger was more interested in the bird than his first and second law. Izmel pointed to the tree, and he said, "no matter how many worms I throw, the bird won't come closer to me".

Munger said, "this is not an ordinary bird! This is the Hoopoe! It is revered in the land of saints and prophets; it was a servant of the king of east. I have traveled all across the southern land and have never seen a Hoopoe neither to the north nor to the south of Chechua." Izmel said, "O' God what have I done! I cried for your help and you showed me this bird, the Hoopoe, servant of the king of the east. I threw stones and cursed him; what sin have I committed! I threw away the gem I had in my hand for I was impatient and too greedy for his love."

Munger said, "Grieve not Izmel, for you have grieved too much in your life. Surely, you have thrown away a gift that God sent to you. But remember God is Most Merciful and you must thank Him for the lesson you have learnt. Only the appreciative succeed in this life and hereafter."

Thus, Izmel wrote his third law, "**be grateful for everything you have, and everything you don't have.**"

Munger continued, "Every being goes through its own struggle. It works hard – willingly or unwillingly – to grow to the shape and form it is. Every being has a unique story and every being has a unique experience. They all grow to the form and shape by their unique circumstances. There are countless beings influencing each other, and there are countless efforts by known and unknown beings to influence each other."

Munger looked at the Hoopoe on the tree and continued,

"Like every being in the world, that Hoopoe has a story – a story before it was born, a story after it was born and a story after it dies. That Hoopoe has perhaps traveled thousands of miles to get here, perhaps crossed the mighty ocean of the east, perhaps missed its flock on its way to somewhere in the North, perhaps it has lost its mate…"

Izmel interrupted, "don't call it 'it', call it 'he'"

Munger apologized for his insensitiveness, and corrected, "Perhaps he has lost his mate."

Munger continued, "it took millions of years to shape that Hoopoe, those feathers, that beak, and his love to his mate. He may not be the most perfect looking Hoopoe in the world, but what is a perfect looking Hoopoe? If every human had one eye, humans would be so used to one eye that if a baby was born with two eyes, humans would pity that baby. Thus, what is perfect? That Hoopoe in the tree is perfect for what it is, feathered or featherless, beaked or beakless, black or orange. You threw stones at him, you cursed him but remember that that Hoopoe is unique, Izmel is unique, and you both have your own stories, for what you have done, and what the Hoopoe has done."

Izmel asked, "If every being in this universe and beyond has its own stories, why should I seek forgiveness? Why can't I just say it is my story that led me to curse the Hoopoe, throw stones at the Hoopoe? How am I responsible for what I did, for it is my story that lead me to be impatient, it is my story that led me to curse and throw stones? Perhaps it was Siempre, perhaps it was a story entangled in me before even I was born? I can't blame Siempre either, because Siempre had a story as well."

Munger said, "you are right, Izmel. You need to understand blame in order to understand forgiveness, for how can forgiveness exist without blame? If you ask for forgiveness without understanding blame, what good is that forgiveness? If you don't understand what you are blaming yourself for, what good is blame?"

Munger proceeded, "In order to understand blame, you need to understand the difference between feelings and actions. In order to understand the difference between feelings and actions, you need to define yourself."

Izmel asked, "Is it pain?"

"when you cut your nails, you don't feel any pain. Is that nail not yours?

"Is it control?"

"Do you think you have control over your heartbeat? Is your heart not yours?

"Is it right?"

"In Chechua and Magua, you could own a man. In the Northern land, you can only rent a man. So, if a man owner from Chechua goes to the Northern land, he will not have right to the man he owns. So, is the man not his?"

Izmel felt very challenged, because he did not know who he was.

"Is it vibrations"?

"When you meditate as per the second tribe, you feel the vibrations. When I meditate as per the second tribe, I feel the vibrations. Is my vibration yours? When you meditate in the woods of happiness you feel vibrations, when you meditate in the jungle of sadness, you feel vibrations, are you the vibration of the woods of happiness or are you the vibration of the jungle of sadness?

Izmel finally gave up and asked,

"Who am I?"

"If I know who you are, then you will be me. Only you can tell who you are"

"Who are you?"

"I am what I think I am. If I think the world is me, then I become the world. I feel pain when stars collide, and volcanos erupt. If I think I am the clan of Chechua, I feel pain when Chechuans die, and I will kill myself fighting for the pride of Chechuans. If I think I am my body, I feel pain when someone says I look ugly, and I feel anxious if I get sick. If I think I am my mind, I feel pain when I am proved wrong, and I feel pain when someone calls me stupid. I am what I think I am. Some call 'what I think I am' as consciousness, the more spiritual ones call it soul. I call it 'what I think I am' or sometimes I call it me."

"So, if I think I am the wealthy fat black lady of the Northern land, will I become the wealthy fat black lady of the Northern land?"

"Yes, you won't look as pretty as her, but you will feel you are as pretty as her. But now since you think you are her body if someone calls you ugly, you will feel pain as bad as you deserve."

"So, if I think I am nothing, then will I become nothing?"

"Yes, you will feel like nothing, but since you still 'think' that you are nothing, you are not nothing – because thinking is not nothing. So, if someone says you are something you will feel pain as bad as you deserve."

Izmel knew there was no sense in arguing with Munger – he thought Munger had either lost all his sense from his travels or was just losing his sanity from his old age.

Izmel said, "okay Munger, do you think you are a Bookman?"

"No, I do not think I am only a Bookman"

"So, when Zerene called you a Bookman, did you feel pain?"

"No, because I think I am a Bookman, I just don't think I am only a Bookman."

"So, who do you think you are?"

Munger said, "I will tell you who I think I am, if you tell me who you think you are"

Izmel said, "I need time. Perhaps, after my travels to the Northern land, I will know who I think I am."

Both nodded their head side to side.

Munger said, "You will know who you are when you know who you are not"

Izmel said, "I know who I am not. I am not a billion things in this world. I am not the star for when I see it is falling down, I do not feel any pain. I am not the worms under the land, for when I chew their heads, I do not feel any pain. I am not my mother"

Lo! Izmel started crying profusely.

Munger went close to him, and asked, "why are you crying O' young man of Magua?"

Izmel could hardly talk – he cried so much that the tears would have flooded the gate of Chechua.

He said, "I am my mother, I am my father, I am the life of my desire. I know my mother is sick, and my father is old – yet I ran away from them for I do not know who I am. I thought I was this mortal body, I thought I was my intellect, but why am I crying when I think of my mother, when I think of my father? I knew not who I was, but I now know who I am. Their pain is my pain, their pain is my pain, my pain is who I am." And Izmel fell down to the ground.

Munger went closer to Izmel and said, "well said, Izmel – now you know who you are but the pain will be quenched only when you accept who you are. Maybe you want to go back to where your heart belongs."

Munger asked, "do you want to go to the South or the North?"

Izmel, after some thought, said, "North."

So Munger gave him some food to eat, a copy of the books of the first tribe, a pack of orange dye and a map to the Northern land.

Izmel was expecting Munger to question his hypocrisy, but Munger didn't utter a word. Both nodded their heads side to side, and Munger left to the South.

Izmel bid farewell to the gate of Chechua, and he looked at the Hoopoe one last time before he headed to the north to know what he knew not.

Chapter 10

The Light – The name after nameless

The sands were clean, the mountains were parched,
- Izmel on his human foot went past the clouds.
His walk was furious, hoarding the knowledge on his back,
his desire to know - to meet the first tribe, the second tribe and
every tribe until he knew what he knew not
(it was only the burden on his human mind)

He ate the cactus, the fungi and worms,
he drank the water for his thirst was dear.
In sands and the mountains, and the woods and goats,
Izmel knew what he wanted to want.

Life as it breaths to soul of his life,
he never went abstained from the spirits of his soul.
Izmel, a step behind, a step ahead,
he knew what he wanted to want.

No shyness would overtake his path,
no courage would pride his feebleness,
Izmel walked with what he had,
seeking what, what he had not.

Suns and moons rose in the land of Chechua,
roosters called the morning prayers,
mothers were waiting for their lost sons,
yet Izmel walked to the Northern land for he yearned for what he wanted to want.

Hoopoe drank the tears on the gate,
Izmel strong on his mission to know,
He had nothing to do but walk to the North to meet the first tribe,
the second tribe and every tribe until he knew what he knew not.

Days and nights passed in the woods,
heat and cold brushed on his skin,
- nothing could stop his human foot,
for he walked where he was destined to walk.

Shadows shortened and lengthened by the shade of sun,
yet Izmel had no thoughts on what brought the light,
until one day he saw the wall covering the rooves,
of the Northern land.

The wall was huge, as high as mountains,
guarded by machines flying and crawling,
thousands of men with orange faces,
looking with eyes as dry as the sand.

Izmel wiped the orange color,
on his face and every part of his skin,
until he saw the first orange man,
on the gates of the southern wall of the Northern land.

Countless women and children were waiting in line to get a step to the Northern land, Izmel stood behind them with his orange face, and his thoughts were nowhere but to what he knew not.

A lady on his front asked him, "you look orange like the men of Northern land, why are you standing on this line? Orange men do not stand and wait like us, they fly high above the wall on the flying machine."

Izmel said, "O' lady on my front, I am here to walk with you, I am here to walk without you."

Having said that Izmel didn't utter another word. He passed through the orange guards like a slimy eel. They asked him a thousand questions, but he did not utter a word. They looked at the book of the first tribe Izmel had and let him walk through the gates of the southern wall of the Northern land. A small step for Izmel, a giant leap for Izmel.

Izmel continued walking to the North – nor the grandeur of the wall behind, nor the amusement of the machines above wavered Izmel's mind. He knew not why the guards let him in, he cared less of anything but what he knew not.

Miles and miles left behind, on the first day of the twenty second month, Izmel met the first tribe. He walked inside the house with the roof of the eggshell and said "O' people of the first tribe, I come to you with many questions. And I know you have answers to many questions. So, what I ask you is many questions, and perhaps you can help me".

Having heard this, the chief of the first tribe said to the guards, "let him in, for maybe we can help this young orange man."

Izmel said, "O chief of the first tribe, who am I? Munger the bookman said I am what I think, yet I left my mother and father, and I am here in the Northern land in the house of the first tribe."

The chief said, "whoever said you are what you think, does not know who he is. His knowledge is his ego, and he is perished by his ego."

"You are not what you think, for you to think, there should be you. If 'you' are what you think, how can 'you' exist without you thinking?"

Izmel said, "well said, O' chief of the first tribe. So, who am I?"

The chief of the first tribe said, "you were born before you were born here. You sinned before you started sinning here. You are a sinful soul who was indecisive when the devil rebelled against God, when the devil thought he could be a god. Didn't you think the devil could be a god? That you could govern yourself? You, me, and every pious soul in this world are sinners. Every human soul is a sinful soul, for if they did not sin, why would they be human?"

Hearing which, every human in the house of the first tribe feared greatly.

Izmel raised his brows so high that they reached to the roof of the eggshell. He definitely didn't recall about the rebellion, but he knew well that he was unlike the Hoopoe and the plants and the stars. So, he asked, "if every human soul sinned so much, why do we have machines that crawl, machines that fly?"

The chief of the first tribe said, "the devil is assigned as the temporary god on earth. He says there is nothing to worry about, nothing to fear because humans can find solutions to their problems. You get sick from your own actions, and the devil says no, you can go to a doctor. The earth is boiling by the smokes of machines, and the devil says no, you can go live outside the earth. You get mad and lunatic with life, and the devil says no, you can go talk to a Shaman. Countries threaten each other with machines that can turn earth into hell, and the devil says, build machines to guard more machines. We continue building and working hard, in an illusion of protecting ourselves – the more we try to protect ourselves, the greater the burden we put on ourselves."

Izmel said, "I suffered greatly in life", and he told his story with Siempre, Zerene and the Hoopoe. Having heard this, some men in the house of the first tribe shouted, "He is a sinner, cast him out or we shall throw stones on him." The chief of the first tribe silenced the men and said, "who is not a sinner here? Rise up if anyone is not a sinner here!"

Hearing this the entire tribe went in silence. The chief of the first tribe continued, "O' young orange man, everyone here has sinned – or else, we wouldn't be born as sane humans. Your suffering from Siempre was sad and great. It was at a tender human age that should not have happened. Your suffering with Zerene and the Hoopoe is sad as well. But remember, you were not five years old when you met Siempre, you had already lived thousands or millions of years before. You are your soul, and the soul was not a child when you met Siempre."

The chief of the first tribe continued, "but, remember you are not me, if it were so we both would have had the same experiences, same worries and the same struggles. There are souls suffering greatly starving for food, there are souls suffering greatly with grapes and wine in their mansions. Some souls were bigger rebels, and others were smaller rebels. The orange and the black, the brown and the yellow, every human soul rebelled against God. It is such a shame for us on earth."

Izmel said, "if I am a soul, and you are a soul, then what is the soul? How big is the soul? Why can't I see it?"

The chief of the first tribe got furious upon hearing this question, he stood up and said loudly "do you think this world is created without purpose? People in the Northern land have found machines that fly and that can burn the earth. They have seen the beauty of nature, the tiny particles that make up existence, and the invisible particles that make up the universes. But they see the beauty in 'how', they never see the beauty in the ultimate 'why'! They learn so much on mind and matter, but they have no answers to why there is mind, why there is matter! Such are the fools of the modern world, who claims they are full of wisdom, but they are the ones who are the biggest fools!"

Izmel thought the chief of the first tribe was playing around with his question. He had asked about the soul, and here he was talking about 'how' and 'why'.

Staying patient, Izmel said, "when I used to play with Siempre, who molded iron into steel, and wired silicon into marvelous lights, his eyes were filled with joy and so were mine. He marveled at how beautifully nature behaved, how marvelously this world is created, and so did I. Is it a sin to marvel at this creation? Is it a sin to fill with tears as we look up at the sky?"

The chief of the first tribe fell in tears, and said "true, there is a beauty to how! True, there is a beauty in how. How beautiful this world is, and how marvelous God's creations are - true, there is a beauty in how. But, the people of the modern world are empty in their hearts, they marvel at the beauty of the creations, they take delight in the beauty of women and machines – there is beauty in how. There is definitely beauty in how."

The head of the chief of the first tribe was humbled, and said, "the beauty in 'how' has taken away the beauty in 'why'. People of the Northern land exclaim 'how beautiful it is', but they rarely think 'why is it beautiful'. What is the purpose of our existence? Why there is this beauty at-all? Why was the universe created? Why do humans toil the soil? Some people of the modern world have their own answers to these questions, and some just don't care – so were the people of the previous generations. Some say these things are all here to help promulgate humankind, the more thoughtful ones say it is in the self-interest of the tiny particles that makes our animal life. Others who explore the universe say, there is no why, because nothingness cannot have a why. The answer is empty no matter how they answer. The emptiness brings great suffering, and some emptiness leads to hopelessness. Many people in the Northern land take their own lives, snort things that take away their souls, all for the sake of emptiness."

It was the sunset of the first day of the twenty second month, and the caller in the house called for prayer upon which everyone in the house washed themselves and turned towards the larger house to pray the evening prayer. Izmel, afraid of washing his face and hands, as he would lose the orange color from his face greatly feared following the first tribe. He sat around the corner when the people of the first tribe prayed. Upon the completion of the prayer, Izmel asked "O' people of the first tribe, why do you pray when there is sunset. Why can't you pray whenever you want?"

The chief of the first tribe said, "the emptiness in the human soul is the breeding ground for the devil. It strangles humans, it kills humans, it deceives humans for lust and greed. The emptiness creates hopelessness and loneliness and men and women fall down as prey of their arrogance. Thus, the people of the first tribe know at the sunset that our lives are not empty for we have a prayer coming up at night. At night we know that the life is not empty for there is a prayer coming in the morning. In the morning we know that life is not empty for there is a prayer coming in the noon, and so on all day long and all year long the people of the first tribe shy away from emptiness which is a breeding ground for devil."

Izmel, content with the answers so far, thanked God for guiding him towards the first tribe. He then asked, "You have talked about 'how', 'why' and emptiness when I asked about soul. I still do not know what the soul is. How big is the soul? Why can't I see it?"

The chief of the first tribe went silent for a while and said "for you to know what soul is, you have to know 'why' you are on the earth, that it is a test, it is the opportunity for you to redeem yourself from your past sins, and God is Most Merciful. It has to be unseen for it is the test."

Izmel asked "So, if the test is why the soul is not seen, why God is not seen? Why do we not remember our rebellious past?"

The chief of the first tribe said, "If the soul was seen how would it be a test? You would know how grown up your soul is, and you would see how grown up other's souls are. You are ashamed to cover up this mortal body with twigs and cotton, so would you want your soul to be shown bare and naked?"

The people of the first tribe were curious for nobody had asked these questions before. They were busy counting nineteens, for their obsession with the 'how' of the nineteen had left them far away from the 'why' of the nineteen. Now a gentile orange man is here, challenging the chief of the first tribe so much that the chief has to bow his head.

"God Most Merciful forgave us and tested our forefather in the paradise. They failed over there as they covered themselves in shame. God Most Merciful forgave them and sent them down to earth. This is the test, our only chance to submit to God, and to admit that we have no power but by the will of God. And as you can see with your bare eyes, we rebel every day for we shall not win until we kill our egos. Tests and temptations come every day, and we fail again and again throughout our lives. Yet, God is Most Merciful and gives us a chance every time we fall prey to our ego, until death from which there is no escape."

"If you see your soul, if you see God, if you remember your past you will fall down trembling in fear - and how would that be a test! The test requires that to be hidden, and that you believe in the test from the signs you are shown. You can marvel at the 'how', think on 'why', or count the nineteen to believe in the signs. The test requires you to believe in the unseen, and fear the unseen and, only a few of the millions of humans on earth will pass the test to submit to God."

People in the house of the first tribe had heard much for the day and were running out of patience. One man rose up and said, "let's count nineteens for we haven't had time to count nineteens today". Another woman rose up and said, "I am afraid we are losing time here for we could have glorified God all night long". The chief of the first tribe had nothing much to say, so they got back to counting nineteens. Izmel walked out of the house, to the city where the cactus grows as tall as mountains.

He looked high at the stars and said, "God, I see the stars high above, many stable, while some fall down the sky. I see the cactus as tall as mountains, I see the darkness at the horizon. Yet, when the test comes, I fail miserably. I failed with Siempre, I failed with Zerene and I failed with the Hoopoe. I failed before I was born, and I failed after I was born. I fear if I will fail after I die. O' God please give me strength to resist the temptations and leave my will to you in full. Nothing happens but by your will, yet I fall prey to the temptations of the devil. How can I change my human nature? How can I be better when my soul is rebellious by nature?"

Then he opened the book of the first tribe and read, "Their example in the Gospel is like a seed stretching its shoots until it becomes strong and thick, well balanced upon its stem – pleasing the sowers."

Izmel thus said, "I am a twig, weaker than the windows of the shattered buildings. I need to grow and strengthen my soul. I need to cast away my shyness and believe in God with strength. When the devil comes and says, "Izmel you are a man, you have this body, you deserve to fulfill these temptations", I need to say "yes, I'm a man, my forefather did not see his body, but you duped him and he saw his body, and was covered with shame. I have faith in God to overcome these temptations." Then, when the devil says, "you are a coward, you run away from temptation. If you are supported by God, if you are strong, fight my temptation, win over it and you may attain salvation", I need to say, "my purpose in life is to kill my ego, what will you fight with if I kill my ego?" The devil might come back and say, "you are missing so much in this beautiful life, there are beautiful women and wonderful machines. Why are you killing this ego you are given?". Then I need to say, "I have a soul and there are two sides to it. There are things that I can do without harm, and there are things that I can do with harm. I will choose the former one, for the latter one is my ego."

Having thought this out, Izmel had a much clearer mind. He knew secrets of his own self that he was not aware of. He knew that the soul has two sides, an ego and the good side: the subtle soul. Knowing this, he couldn't wait till the morning when he could go to the house of the first tribe to inform them of this news.

Chapter 11

The Subtle – Wisdom from within

Izmel spent the night under the cactus, and as the morning prayer was called from the house of the first tribe, he rushed in to share his meditation.

Fearless, he washed himself and joined the prayer with the chief of the first tribe. After the prostration, Izmel rose up and said, "I am Izmel from the land of Magua, you can see my true color today for I do not fear anything but the God of the first tribe".

Everyone looked at him in amazement, for they had been fooled by the color of his orange skin. Someone from the tribe stood up and said, "betrayer!" An orange man from the tribe rose up and said, "you have deceived us by the color of your skin!"

As the anger rose in the morning, the chief of the first tribe fell in silence. Izmel, not knowing what to do, opened the first book of the first tribe and read, "the garment of righteousness is the best". One woman stood up and said, "well said Izmel from the land of Magua, but how did you get our first book?". Izmel thus explained how he met Munger the bookman, his journey to the

Northern land, how he met someone from the first tribe and how he got the book."

Izmel said, "I am sorry for hiding my skin, but remember the brother of the eleven brothers hid his golden cup in his brother's bag to proclaim him a thief. Was the brother of eleven brothers not righteous? I had painted myself orange to get to the Northern land, for my idea was deceptive but my intent was good."

Hearing this, everyone went silent. Izmel said, "I meditated last night under the stars, under the cactus. I have found something that I want to share with you."

"I realized that the soul has two sides – the ego and the subtle. Every feeling that God created can be spent in two ways – the ego and the subtle ways. For nothing is bad, and everything can be bad."

The chief of the first tribe said, "yes, every soul has a devil companion, the one who persuades the soul to temptation. If the soul wins over the devil companion, then the soul attains salvation."

Izmel said, "Okay, but the important thing is when temptation comes it can be spent in a good or bad way. The good way is the subtle way, and the bad way is the egotistic way. If you fight the temptation, you will often fail for the temptation as temptation is too hard for human souls to resist. If it was easy, we would not be on earth at all! What we can instead do is to turn to the subtle way, and there is a subtle way for every temptation, as much as there is an egotistic way for every temptation!"

Many people in the house of the first tribe agreed, but the rebellious ones said, "O' Izmel from the land of Magua, we know so much that we don't need your innovations. Do not corrupt us with your new thoughts, for we are here to purify ourselves"

Izmel said, "I will come back to you if I find a better solution, for our common goal is not to be among the losers"

Having said that, Izmel bid farewell to the chief of the first tribe and prayed.

Chapter 12

The companion – On how to conquer

As Izmel bid farewell and walked out of the door of the room with the roof of an eggshell, the chief rushed out to say some final words to Izmel.

The chief said, "my apologies for the arrogance of some of our brothers, but I want to tell you about our devil companions."

Izmel said, "you don't have to apologize, for every soul under the roof or outside the roof are sinful, or else they wouldn't be on earth."

The chief said, "well said, Izmel. You have come a long way!"

"Remember that when the devil rebelled against God, some souls agreed with him, while some souls were indecisive. Those who agreed with devil that they could be independent are cast to devil bodies – they have great powers, made out of fire, although invisible to us. Those who were indecisive that they could be independent are cast to human bodies – they are weak, made out of earth. Whenever a human body is born with a human soul in it, a devil body is born with a devil soul in it, and the devil wanders with us wherever we go."

"Imagine two people, one weak with an indecisive mind, always in self-doubt, and the other powerful, convinced that it is powerful and independent of God, walking together hand in hand, shoulder beside shoulder. One would say, "O' human you can build a palace as high as mountains to protect yourself from wind and hails", and the other would say, "no I am weak as flesh, I can't move a rock with my hand, how can I build a castle?" One would say, "O' human you are strong and beautiful, you can go and fetch that woman's hand", and the other would say "no I am not good enough, I am not sure if I want that woman, I am confused." This battle keeps going, and humans, not knowing what the mind is, study it in great detail, Shamans name it greed, pleasure, jealousy and thousand other names, confused, bewildered – humans are oblivious to what they are."

Izmel asked, "are you saying that being confident like the devil is wrong? How would there be machines that fly and machines that crawl if humans did not listen to devils"?

The chief of the first tribe said, "being confident in your independence is opposite to being submissive. Submission is acceptance of God's fate, not to doubt that we are powerless, not to doubt that only God has all power, not to doubt that God is running everything, including devils. Submission is opposite to confidence. The king of the east had hoopoes and devils working for him, he built great castles, but by the will of God. Machines loftier than what you see can be built in submission, knowledge greater than what you think can be learnt through submission, submission is not being confident in your independence, submission is being confident that nothing can be done except by the will of God."

Izmel hearing this, felt in silence, and asked, "how can we conquer the devil companion?"

The chief of the first tribe said, "there is only one way you can conquer the devil, or even make the devil submit with you. That is why the angels were asked to prostrate on the human body, which is weak as earth, but it can blow the fire with knowledge. The way is to carefully listen to every whisper of the devil companion, listen, and you will know it comes in various forms, various suggestions. Listen, and you will recognize it, coming to you while you are asleep and awake. Listen to voice of your devil companion, for it can be strong or mild. It hits you at your weakest point, if you are easily seduced by women it tempts you there, if you easily gets angry it tempts you there, if you easily get sad, it tempts you there – for whatever the names Shamans call, the devil is trying to say you are independent of God, and you have your own power."

Izmel was confused, "O' chief of the first tribe, what are you saying? Can't I plan my life where it wants to go?"

The chief of the first tribe said, "listen to it! That is the thought of your devil companion. You have been rebellious, your devil companion knows where your weakness is, and you are questioning your dependency on God. This is what you did before you were born."

Izmel fell in shame, and said "O' chief of the first tribe, you saved me this time by the will of God, but how can I save myself when I am alone?"

The chief of the first tribe said, "thank God that I could help you. Proofs. Proofs will help you. What are proofs? When the brother of eleven brothers was seduced by the wife of his master, he almost succumbed to her, she almost succumbed to him. But he saw a proof! It was not his power that saved him from the sin, for there are people saying "O' the brother of the eleven brothers was so good that he stopped himself from sin". Fools! The brother of the eleven brothers had no power, except what God gave him. He was saved by the will of God, the Most Merciful."

"When the man who spoke the gospel spoke from the crib and healed the lepers, people said, "O' he is our lord, perhaps he can help us from the miseries". Fools! The man who spoke the gospel had no power, except what God gave him. Fools believe that humans have power, for they are not submitters and end up with perpetual misery spiraling down their spines".

Having heard this, Izmel was very happy, yet his question remained, "If I understand you right, O' chief of the first tribe, if you submit to God, believe that God runs everything, God will bring you proofs so that the devil companion cannot tempt you."

The chief of the first tribe said, "well said Izmel, listen! For God did not let you learn the names of everything for nothing. Listen! Listen to your devil companion and listen to the proofs. If you are veiled, no matter if the earth shakes, or the clouds fall, you will not see the proof right in front of you. Listen! O' Izmel, listen! Listen to both the sides, listen to the whispers and proofs, and if you submit, you will see them. You will see the proof from a sneaky ant crawling on your foot, you will see the proof from the tiny tone from the wings of a mosquito, you will see the proof from the air as it touches the hair of your nostril, you will see the proof even in the darkness, even in the emptiness devoid of any apparent evidence."

Izmel said, O' Chief of the first tribe, "now having learnt this mystery, what shall I do? How shall I develop these skills?"

The chief of the first tribe said, "Submit, Izmel! Submit! A leaf of a tree does not fall without the will of God. I am afraid of your questions, for I fear your questions will lead you astray. Izmel, you came here by the will of God, you will walk from here by the will of God. You were born by the will of God; you will die by the will of God. You learnt this by the will of God, you will develop the skills by the will of God. How can you ask me "how shall I develop the skills", after listening so much? Remember, you are not developing anything, except by the will of God. If God wills, you will develop, if God wills, you will not develop."

Izmel said, "O' chief of the first tribe. Thank you for your thoughts. I have learnt from you many things by the will of God. I have learnt about souls, companions, whispers, proofs and submission. I also realize that one can hear the whispers and see the proofs through practice. Hence, O' Chief of the first tribe, I will spend time listening to my companions and looking for proofs by the will of God. I will spend time by the will of God as I travel in the Northern land to accept the will of God as it happens."

The chief of the first tribe said, "Northern land is land which no man has ever seen before this age. It is the land of great temptation, yet with great adherence to its principles. Many temptations will pass by, and many proofs - lend your years in humility, and keep your eyes wide open in pittance. You can grow to great heights, if God wills - or, you will fall to the pit of fire."

With that warning, the chief of the first tribe said peace, Izmel shook his head, and they departed for their own chosen destinies.

Chapter 13

Slumber – When the dreams look real

As Izmel bid farewell to the first tribe, he walked with a load on his back, a load heavier than ever before, a load of knowledge, encrypted in the solace of thoughts and ideas. The load on the tender soul was so much that Izmel did not know whether to carry it or shed it in the land where the cactus grew as tall as mountains. He chose to carry it, as far as he could, not knowing where his destiny was and how to practice it.

Knowledge is like a weapon - one can have the sharpest sword on the face of earth, but if he cannot lift it with his arm, or know how to use it, for what good is the sword for? - a heavy burden one would carry, not knowing how to use it. So is wealth, one may heap gold as tall as mountains, but for what good is the gold for if one does not know to use it. Izmel, leaving with the knowledge of the first tribe, had so much to know, so much to tell - yet he did not know how to use it.

The land was still dry, the cactus became scarce, and the sky became bluer as Izmel walked to the north to the heart of the Northern land. He did not see a single Hoopoe, nor any fat dark women, nor any places with cooked meatloaf in between two breads, nor any rich men with cloth tied on their necks! Izmel wondered "what am I here for? Was Munger telling the truth?". Every step he took, Izmel became increasingly skeptical. He was full of doubt until finally he could not take a step further. Exhausted, he fell down to ground, his face tendered by the fine red soil, and he fell asleep.

As the stillness of slumber approached the blood, Izmel gripped his hand to the earth. Who would want to sleep, let their dear soul go away from them when men bleed blood for a dime of gold? Every night when the souls are taken, the world of dreams allures the mind – for if men were not seduced by the whispers of the world of dreams, who would want to let their soul go?

As the dream sneaked into Izmel's mind, no thought could conquer him, nor his reason. He dreamt of an arrow that would break the barrier of the seed, the seed spurting out what was inside. Izmel opened his eyes to the scorching heat, his face sprinkled with the fine red soil of the heart of Northern land. He opened his eyes with hope and fear. He pushed himself against the pull of earth, and as he stood, he saw glimpses of water at a distance. He ran to fetch some water in the mirage of earth, until he saw nothing but sand – sand, that brushed his feet in dismay.

Illusion, Izmel thought. "If earth could fool me with glimpses of water, why not the moon and the sun? If sleep could fool me with glances of dreams, why not life?"

Thus, Izmel knew the profound truth that this universe, this life, the wind and water, the Hoopoe and Zerene, Siempre, his heart and mind – nothing he had seen or smelled is no more than an illusion

Chapter 14
Reality – The causes of illusion

The reality is unseen, the creator is unseen, angels and devils are unseen, even your own soul is unseen! What you see is not what is unseen. Unseen is far more than what is seen, but we dwell on the seen as much as we think there is no unseen. How strange are humans, who believe in the seen but not the unseen, whereas the seen is an illusion and unseen is the real.

Izmel kept walking in the world that is seen, with the emotions and mind littering around what is seen. Izmel kept walking, he forgot he was an unseen soul residing in a seen body. He forgot that he was in an unseen reality walking on a seen universe. Thus, Izmel came back to the reality of illusion, with a million tests written on his destiny. The illusion is thus a test, a test that will lead to a reality of pain or contentment. The pain, they call it hell, and the soul which cannot stand the happiness of contentment walks to hell by itself. The soul that cannot stand the pain of greed walks to heaven. Thus, no one drives anyone, everyone drives themselves until the law is fulfilled.

END OF BOOK ONE

Printed in Poland
by Amazon Fulfillment
Poland Sp. z o.o., Wrocław

63733121R00061